Children of the World

ballel

A Child of Senegal

by Alain Gioanni

BLACKBIRCH PRESS
An imprint of Thomson Gale, a part of The Thomson Corporation

Detroit • New York • San Francisco • San Diego • New Haven, Conn • Waterville, Maine • London • Munich

© Éditions PEMF, 2000

First published by PEMF in France as *Ballel, enfant du Sénégal*.

First published in North America in 2005 by Thomson Gale.

Thomson and Star Logo are trademarks and Gale and Blackbirch Press are registered trademarks used herein under license.

For more information, contact
Blackbirch Press
27500 Drake Rd.
Farmington Hills, MI 48331-3535
Or you can visit our Internet site at http://www.gale.com

ALL RIGHTS RESERVED.
No part of this work covered by the copyright hereon may be reproduced or used in any form or by any means—graphic, electronic, or mechanical, including photocopying, recording, taping, Web distribution or information storage retrieval systems—without the written permission of the publisher.

Every effort has been made to trace the owners of copyrighted material.

Photo Credits: All photos © Alain Gioanni except page 6 © Ariadne Van Zandbergen/Lonely Planet Images; page 8 (large) © Nic Bothma/EPA/Landov; page 9 © Vince Streano/CORBIS; Table of Contents collage: EXPLORER/Boutin (upper left); François Goalec (upper middle and right); Muriel Nicolotti (bottom left); CIRIC/Michel Gauvry (bottom middle); CIRIC/Pascal Deloche (bottom right)

LIBRARY OF CONGRESS CATALOGING-IN-PUBLICATION DATA

Gioanni, Alain.
  Ballel : a child of Senegal / by Alain Gioanni.
    p. cm. — (Children of the world)
  ISBN 1-4103-0285-7 (hardcover : alk. paper)
  1. Senegal—Social life and customs—Juvenile literature. 2. Children—Senegal—Social life and customs—Juvenile literature. I. Title. II. Series: Children of the world (Blackbirch Press)

  DT549.8.G56 2005
  966.305'2—dc22
                                2005000697

Printed in the United States of America
10 9 8 7 6 5 4 3 2 1

Contents

Facts About Senegal 5
Senegal 6
Living off the Waters 8
In Ballel's Home 10
Ballel's Family 12
Ballel's School 14
Games 16
Shopping for Food 18
Making Dinner 20
The Market 22
Other Books in the Series 24

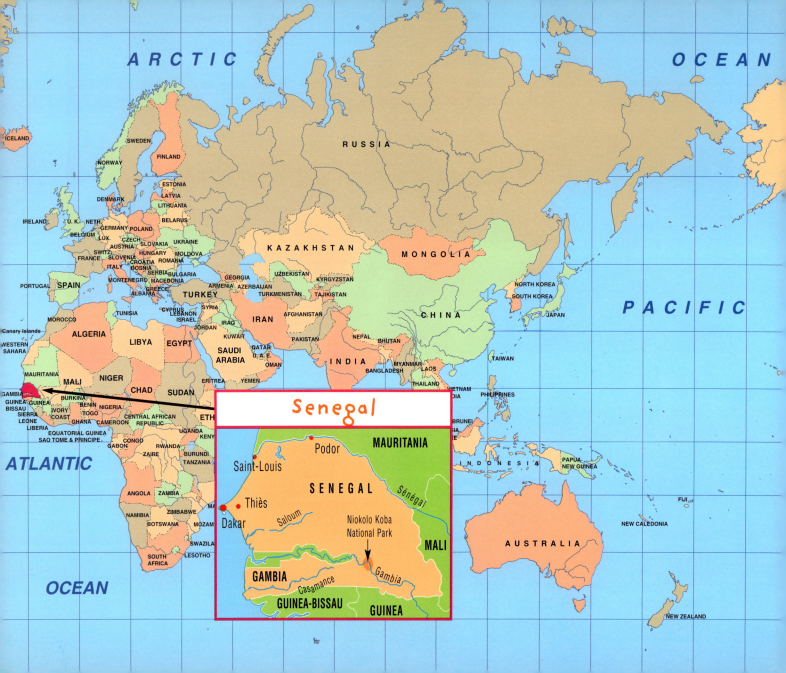

Facts About Senegal

Agriculture:	peanuts, millet, corn, sorghum, rice, cotton
Capital:	Dakar
Government:	republic
Independence:	August 20, 1960
Industry:	food and fish processing, phosphate mining, fertilizer
Land area:	75,749 square miles (196,722 square kilometers)
Languages:	French (official), Wolof, Serere, Pulaar, Diola, Mandinka, Soce
Money:	the CFA franc
Natural resources:	fishing, tourism, phosphates, iron ore, farmland
Population:	10,095,000
Religions:	Muslim (94 percent), Catholic (5 percent), Animism

Senegal

Senegal is a small country on the Atlantic coast of Africa.

Fishing boats bring fresh fish to the beach market of Pétite Côte in Thiès province, Senegal.

It lies between the desert and the tropical jungles. Another small country, Gambia, cuts right down the middle of Senegal.

Senegal has been independent since 1960. Its capital, Dakar, has 2,200,000 inhabitants.

The Gambia River crosses the Niokolo-Koba National Park.

Dakar, the capital of Senegal.

Living off the Waters

The Senegalese eat a lot of fish. They brave the ocean in brightly colored open boats called pirogues to catch the fish.

Right: Eight hundred pirogues are ready for fishing.

Left: Tourists come to Senegal to enjoy the beaches and the friendly people.

Below: The Pink Lake.

Pink Lake is situated a few hundred feet from the sea, near Dakar. It gets its name because of its color. The Senegalese collect salt from it.

Many tourists come to Dakar to enjoy the beaches. They also discover the different landscapes and the life of the people.

In Ballel's Home

Ballel is a seven-year-old girl. She was born on the banks of the Senegal River, in a little village in the bush. Today, she lives in Thiès, 37 miles (60 kilometers) from Dakar.

Left: Ballel and her mother.

Below: Ballel's house and the papaya trees in the courtyard.

Ballel lives in a house made of bricks and cement. Her house has electricity and a telephone. The water faucet is in the courtyard, at the foot of a papaya tree.

Washing day.

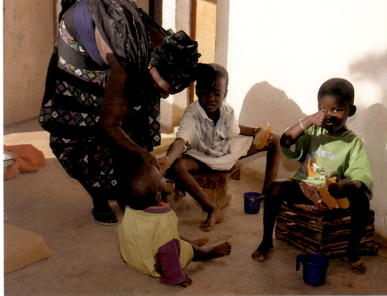

Inside the house, Ballel is pictured with her mother and brothers.

Many of Ballel's neighbors do not have running water and have to go to the well for water. But Ballel and her mother can do their laundry in the courtyard.

Ballel's Family

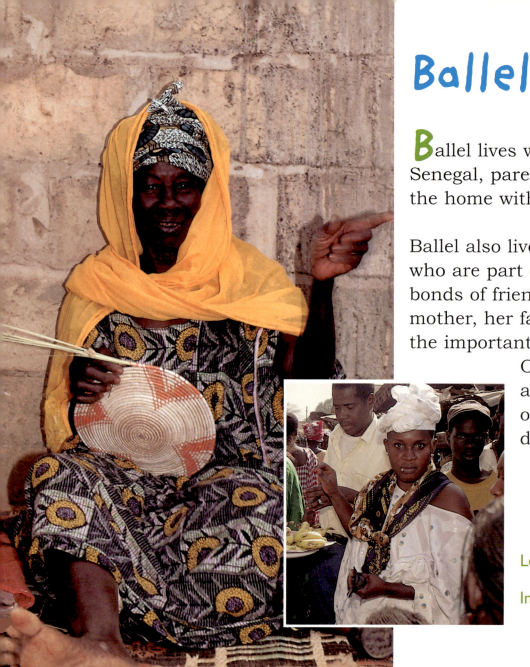

Ballel lives with her family. In Senegal, parents and children share the home with uncles and cousins.

Ballel also lives with other people who are part of her family due to bonds of friendship. Her grandmother, her father's mother, holds the important position of ancestor. Others often ask her for advice. She takes care of the children and does crafts.

Left: Ballel's grandmother.

Inset: Aicha, Ballel's mother.

Ballel's father teaches classes about agriculture. Her two little brothers are named Abdoulaye and Malick.

Abdoulaye, Ballel's brother.

Above: Ballel's father.

Below: Malick, Ballel's youngest brother.

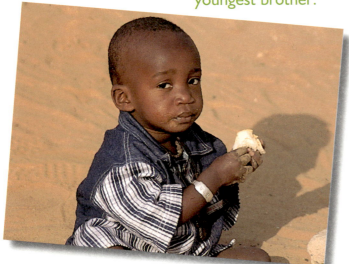

Ballel's School

Left: Ballel crosses the street to her school.

Below: Ballel's teacher and his class.

Ballel's teacher must teach 120 students! He divides his class into two groups of 60. Ballel goes to school only on Monday and Friday mornings and Tuesday and Thursday afternoons.

Ballel in class.

In class, Ballel sits with two other children at a desk built for only two.

As in classrooms throughout the world, the blackboard is an important part of Ballel's class.

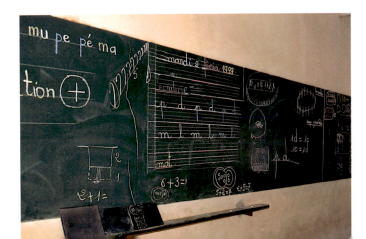

Ballel is in the first grade. The class is taught in French. Ballel has only one book for all subjects.

Ballel is a good student who works hard on her homework. Of course, she would rather play with her friends!

In the evening, Ballel does her homework.

Games

Ballel spends a lot of time in the streets of her neighborhood. She plays with Abdoulaye and Malick, and with her friends.

In Africa, children cannot buy toys. They make their own toys with whatever they can, such as wire, cloth, the soles of shoes, and tin cans.

African children make many kinds of toys: cars, animals, hoops, and vehicles to pull and push.

The street is the playground for the children.

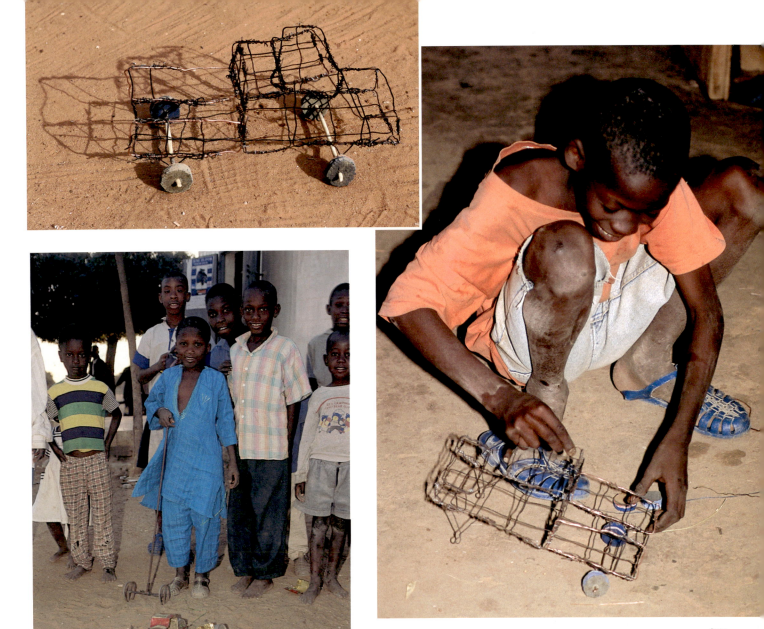

Parsley.

Shopping for Food

Sometimes Ballel goes with her mother, Aicha, to the market at the other end of town. They go there by bus.

Aicha fills her bucket with the ingredients for thiébou diène, a kind of stew they will have for their midday meal. She buys carrots, cabbage, squash, and fish.

Cabbages.

Fish.

19

Making Dinner

Back at home, Ballel and her mother begin preparing the thiébou diène.

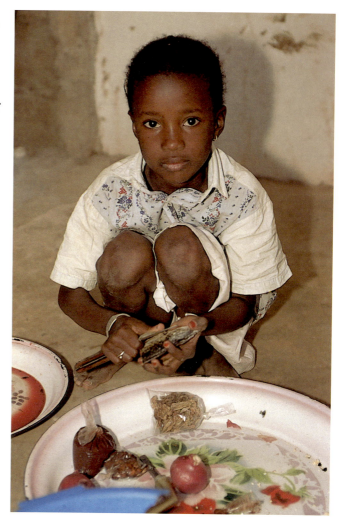

Above: Ballel scales the fish.

Left: Aicha sifts the rice.

They must scale the fish and sort the rice to remove stones. When the stew is ready, the children eat it with their grandmother.

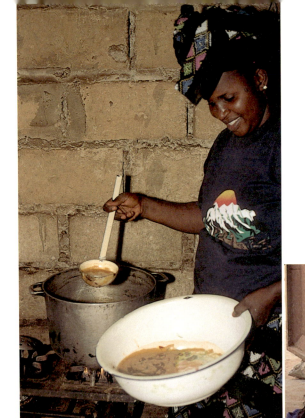

Above: Aicha cooks and prepares the sauce.

The Market

This market has everything, including food, cloth, pots, and pans. There are also some products that you may not recognize such as bitter eggplants, okra, and hot peppers . . .

These pots are made from aluminum that has been recycled from old car motors.

Tamarind pods.

Manioc.

Peppers.

Artisans sell their crafts on the sidewalk. Here, the tailor is working out in the open.

. . . and other things you can discover in these photos.

For dessert, there are bananas that are grown locally. They are smaller but much sweeter than the ones you are used to eating.

Bissap, dried hibiscus flowers, are used to make a drink, and peanuts.

Other Books in the Series

Arafat: A Child of Tunisia
Asha: A Child of the Himalayas
Avinesh: A Child of the Ganges
Basha: A Hmong Child
Frederico: A Child of Brazil
Ituko: An Inuit Child

Kradji: A Child of Cambodia
Kuntai: A Masai Child
Leila: A Tuareg Child
Madhi: A Child of Egypt
Thanassis: A Child of Greece
Tomasino: A Child of Peru

Ballel.

16 32